You Know It!

SAMMY
the Steiger

Gotcha!

FRANKIE
the Farmall

Got___

CODY
the Combine

Hey Dudes!

BAILEY
the Baler

Go Team!

KELLIE
the Combine

Awesome!

PETER
the Patriot Sprayer

VROOM!

SCOOTER
the Case IH Scout

Let's Do It!

TAMMI
the Tiller

Details!

EVAN
the Early Riser Planter

This book belongs to:

Name: _ _ _ _ _ _ _ _ _ _ _ _ _ _ _ _ _ _

Favorite type of cow: _ _ _ _ _ _ _ _ _ _

Busy on the Farm
with Casey & Friends

It's a beautiful morning at Happy Skies Farm. The hay is ready to be baled — and just in time. The weather forecast calls for rain.

We'd better get moving. Casey and the team have busy days ahead. Let's go!

Farm Crops

Farmers grow different crops that can be baled into hay. Hay is grasses and legume plants used to feed livestock, or farm animals, such as cows, sheep, and horses.

ALFALFA

DEALER

RED CLOVER

SORGOM-SUDANGRASS

HYBRID

PERRENIAL GRASSES

GRASS-LEGUME

MIX

The type of crop a farmer grows for hay depends on three things: climate, what the hay is used for, and how much hay it will make.

SEED

Preparing Hay

There are many steps to haymaking. The first step is to mow, or cut, the hay. After the hay is cut, it is left to dry in the field. Finally, when the hay is almost completely dry, it's raked into rows, called windrows. Now, it's ready to be baled.

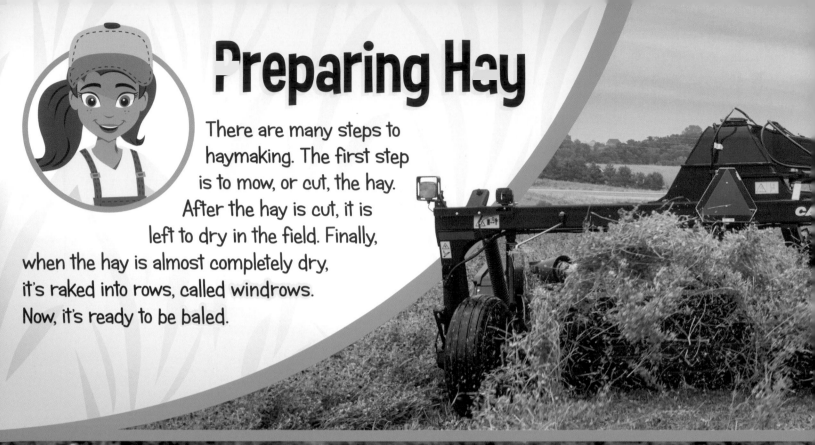

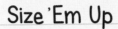
Size 'Em Up

Hay can be baled in square or round shapes of different sizes.

Small bales feed fewer animals.

Large bales feed lots of animals.

Did You Know?

Hay and straw are not the same thing! Hay is grown specifically as hay. Straw is what's left of a plant after the grain has been harvested.

Making Round Bales

Once hay is mowed, dried, and raked into windrows, it's ready to be baled. Here's how it works!

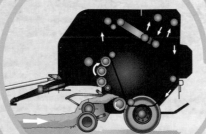

Step 1

Step 2

The tractor and baler travel over the windrows.

The baler picks up hay from the windrow and feeds it into the bale chamber. Belts grip the hay and carry it upward to the core forming area.

Step 3

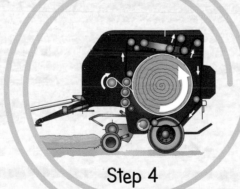

Step 4

Step 5

Rollers begin curling the hay to form the center. The bale continues to rotate and grow as more hay is added.

When the bale is the right size, the farmer stops the tractor. Net or twine wraps around the bale to keep it from falling apart.

The tailgate opens and ejects the wrapped bale.

7

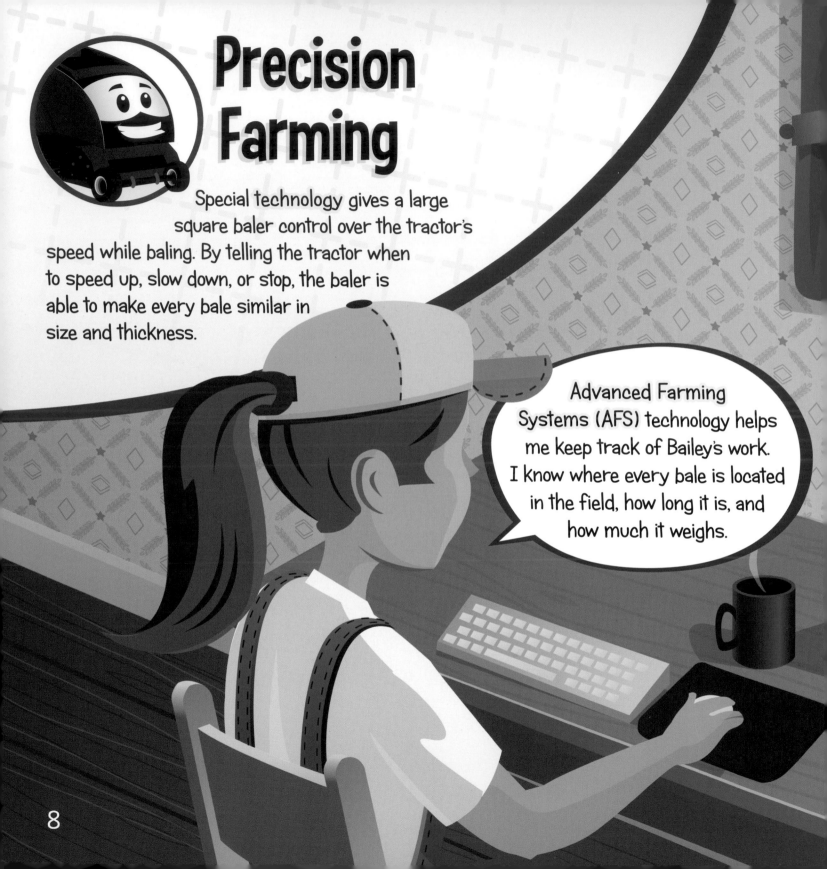

Precision Farming

Special technology gives a large square baler control over the tractor's speed while baling. By telling the tractor when to speed up, slow down, or stop, the baler is able to make every bale similar in size and thickness.

Advanced Farming Systems (AFS) technology helps me keep track of Bailey's work. I know where every bale is located in the field, how long it is, and how much it weighs.

8

TILLUS TALK

Moving Bales

Since bales are dropped in the field, other equipment is needed to move them.

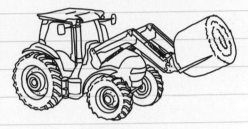

Large tractors move bales onto trailers.

Pickup trucks move small trailers to storage.

Semitrucks move large trailers long distances.

Farm Buildings

Barns and sheds are designed especially for animals, equipment, crops, and bales.

Big doors allow equipment to move in and out.

Windows help fresh air flow through the building.

Stalls give each animal space to eat and sleep.

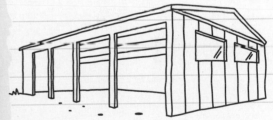

Did You Know?

The first barns were colored red from rust that was added to an oil mixture used to protect the wood.

11

The Perfect Utility Tractor

Tractors come in different sizes and power ranges. Farmers depend on small utility tractors—like Frankie and Fern—for everyday chores.

Gearing Up For Work

Farmall tractors have special features that power and pull different types of tools, called attachments. Using the right attachment helps make tasks easier and faster to complete.

NAME	FRANKIE
EQUIPMENT	LOADER
ATTACHMENT	BUCKET

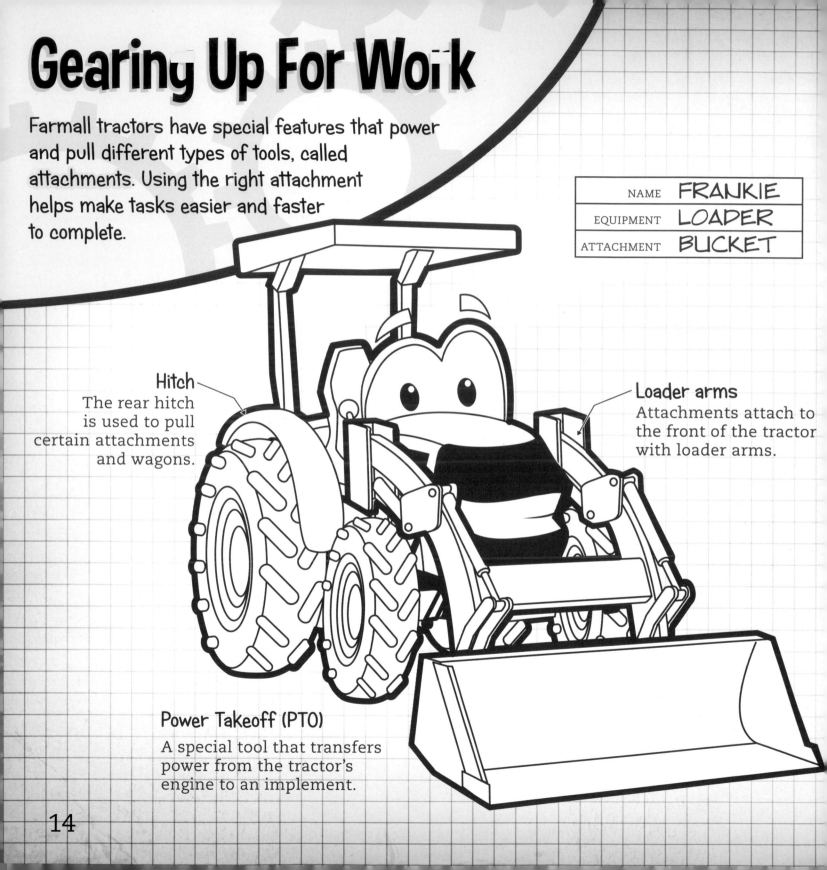

Hitch
The rear hitch is used to pull certain attachments and wagons.

Loader arms
Attachments attach to the front of the tractor with loader arms.

Power Takeoff (PTO)
A special tool that transfers power from the tractor's engine to an implement.

14

Rotary cutter
mows grass

Post hole digger
digs holes quickly

Snow blower
clears snow from
sidewalks and drives

Blade
moves or levels sand,
dirt, snow, and gravel

Mower conditioner
cuts and dries crops

Manure spreader
spreads manure
on fields

Boom arm mower
trims grass around
ditches and waterways

Snow plow
removes snow and ice

Bucket
loads, carries, and
dumps materials like
grain, manure, and soil

Bale grip
moves and stacks
bales

Pallet fork
lifts pallets of heavy
objects

Bale spear
moves and stacks
bales

15

Working for the City

Small tractors aren't just for the farm. Cities and towns use them to mow the sides of roads, dig holes and ditches, clean beaches, and work with garbage and recycling.

Small tractors even help out at the golf course and at parks!

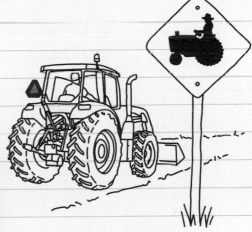
17

Maintaining the Farm

Casey relies on me to keep the farm in top condition. I spread gravel on roads, dig ditches and holes for better drainage, and clear brush and fallen trees. And that's just the beginning! I am a "Frankie-of-all-trades."

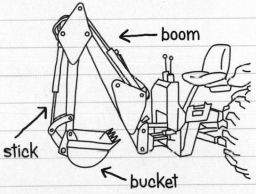

Backhoe Science

Frankie uses a backhoe to dig up hard material or lift heavy loads.

A backhoe is made of three parts: *boom*, *stick*, and *bucket*.

← boom

stick

← bucket

These parts move like your arm or finger.

Did You Know?

The name *backhoe* comes from the action of the shovel. It digs by pulling the bucket backward.

19

Working with Animals

I take care of the animals for Casey. My bale spear helps move hay to feed the cows and horses. And my bucket carries clean straw for fresh bedding. I love keeping the animals happy and healthy!

TILLUS TALK

Make Haste with that Waste!

Where there are farm animals, there is waste. And lots of it!

Farmers make a waste management plan.

The plan explains how the farmer will get rid of the waste.

POO.

Did You Know?

A waste management plan includes guessing how much waste will be made, how it will be stored, and where it will end up.

Cattle breeds are divided into two groups: dairy and beef. Dairy cows give us milk and beef cattle give us meat.

Holstein

The most popular dairy cow in the United States, Holsteins produce more milk than any other dairy breed.

Jersey

One of the oldest dairy breeds, Jerseys are very gentle and easy to manage.

Aryshire

They originally came from Scotland, where the land is rough and weather is cold.

Brown Swiss

Believed to be the oldest dairy breed, Brown Swiss are very gentle in nature.

Guernsey

Named after a tiny island near France, Guernseys produce milk that is high in butterfat and protein.

Angus

Their black color helps keep skin from burning in the sun.

Hereford

Politician Henry Clay was the first to import Herefords to the United States, in 1817.

Texas Longhorn

They are the only cattle breed that has adapted to the North American environment without help from people.

Highland

Known for their long-haired coats, they use their horns to dig through snow for food.

Simmental

Special coloring around the eyes helps to protect them from bright sunlight.

Specialty Farming

Small tractors are useful for different types of farming. Our size allows us to fit between rows of fruit trees in orchards. We're the perfect size to zoom in and out of greenhouse buildings. And we work in vineyards to mow between rows.

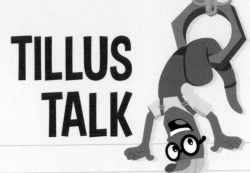
Farmers to the Rescue

Healthy crops require cooperation from Mother Nature.

When extreme weather threatens crops, farmers come to the rescue!

They work around the clock to make sure crops won't be destroyed.

Did You Know?

If temperatures get too cold, grape farmers in Europe build small bonfires in their vineyards to keep the grapevines from freezing.

25

Happy Skies Farm in Numbers

Farming is a business. I keep track of everything I grow, gather, buy, and sell. This information helps me make changes so I can farm better next year.

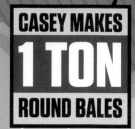

CASEY MAKES 1 TON ROUND BALES

NATIONAL AVERAGE FOR CORN} 168 BUSHELS PER ACRE

1 ACRE PRODUCES 10,000 POUNDS OF ALFALFA PER YEAR

1 COW NEEDS ABOUT 2 ACRES OF PASTURE TO FEED

NATIONAL AVERAGE FOR SOYBEANS **48** BUSHELS PER ACRE

CASEY'S SILOS CAN HOLD UP TO **122,000** BUSHELS OF GRAIN

COWS ARE USUALLY

MILKED 2 TIMES A DAY

1 COW EATS **50** POUNDS OF FOOD EACH DAY!

FOOD

1 COW PRODUCES AROUND 6.5 GALLONS OF MILK EACH DAY!

All in the Family

Since 1923, Farmall tractors have worked hard to help farmers. Lots of famous people—and even some presidents!—have relied on our power.

Our family is so special that modern farmers collect old Farmall tractors. Even Casey has her great-grandfather's Farmall M!

GLOSSARY

ADVANCED FARMING SYSTEMS (AFS)

special technology in Case IH tractors used to help farmers do their job

ATTACHMENTS

tools that go on a tractor and are used for special jobs

BALE

a large bundle of hay tightly tied together

BALE SPEAR

a tool that goes on a tractor and is used to move hay bales

BREED

a group within each animal type that has a common origin and each member looks very similar

CLIMATE

the usual weather patterns of a particular place

EJECT

to push something out

LEGUME

a plant that has seeds that grow in long cases

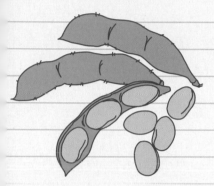

LIVESTOCK

animals that are raised by farmers

ORCHARD

a place where fruit trees are grown

ROTATE

to move or turn in a circle

TECHNOLOGY

equipment created by science to solve a problem

UTILITY

something created to be useful

VINEYARD

a place that grows grapes

WINDROW

hay that is cut and raked into rows

FUN FACTS!

Cows are part of the Bovinae subfamily, which includes buffalo, yaks, and antelopes!

Farmall was the first tractor in the United States with a tricycle design.

The first Farmall tractors were gray until they changed the color to Red #50.

Farmers measure milk in pounds.

A cow's stomach has 4 compartments.

Rumen

Omasum

A dairy cow can produce 120 pounds of waste a day.

Reticulum

Abomasum

Large 5×6 round bales weigh between 500 to 2,200 pounds and are the most popular size bales in North America.

Octane Press, Edition 1.2 (Hardcover), September 2023
Edition 1.1 (Softcover), November 2022
Edition 1.0 (Hardcover), April 2017

Library of Congress Cataloging-in-Publication Data

ISBN-13: 9781937747794 ISBN-10: 1937747794

1. Juvenile Nonfiction—Transportation—General. 2. Juvenile Nonfiction—Lifestyles—Farm and Ranch Life.

3. Juvenile Nonfiction—Lifestyles—Country Life. 4. Juvenile Nonfiction—Concepts—Seasons

Library of Congress Control Number: 2016949135

Additional photography with permission from Hoard's Dairyman p. 22,
The American Highland Cattle Association (Highland) p. 23,
The American Simmental Association (Simmental) p. 23,
Drovers Magazine: Sara Brown (Angus and Herefords) p. 23,
Drovers Magazine: Wyatt Bechtel (Longhorn) p. 23
and The Wisconsin Historical Society p. 28 (ID25322).

A very special thank you to:
Farm Journal Media
Erin Daluge, *Rock County Agriculture Ambassador*
Dakotah Walker, *Case IH Marketing Department Intern*
Katie Kracht, *Case IH Marketing Department Intern*

octanepress.com

Printed in China

Farming keeps me busy, but I love my life!

CASEY
the Farmer

Casey depends on me for the daily weather report!

TILLUS
the Worm

Easy Peasy!

FERN
the Farmall

Be Ready!

BIG RED
the Magnum